Published by Lion Children's Books
an imprint of
Lion Hudson plc
Wilkinson House, Jordan Hill Road,
Oxford OX2 8DR, England
www.lionhudson.com/lionchildrens

ISBN 978 0 7459 6107 1 (paperback)
ISBN 978 0 7459 6204 7 (hardback)
ISBN 978 0 7459 6344 0 (board book)
ISBN 978 0 7459 6402 7 (mini hardback)
e-ISBN 978 0 7459 6767 7

First edition 2009
This edition 2013

A catalogue record for this book is available
from the British Library

Printed and bound in China, October 2012,
LH17

The Biggest Thing
in the World

Kenneth Steven

Illustrated by
Melanie Mitchell

LION
CHILDREN'S

Little Snow Bear had been fast asleep for 97 and a half days. Now spring time was coming at last. He peeped out of the den to look at the great big world.

Feeling brave, he crept out to the edge of a sparkling pool.

There was his reflection. How very small he looked!

"Come with me, Little Snow Bear," his mother said. She walked with long, lazy strides, and he had to run to catch up with her. He ran so quickly that he tumbled right down a hole in the snow.

"Help," he squeaked.

At once, a paw as big as he was scooped him up and set him down, as softly as a snowflake.

"Be careful," his mother
whispered.

They had set off again, more slowly,
when suddenly they saw a huge
musk ox.

The musk ox snorted and stamped.
As the two bears walked around the
great creature, Little Snow Bear whispered
to his mother, "Is that the biggest thing in the
world?"
But his mother shook her head.

Not long after, they heard a noise, and all at once hundreds and hundreds of elk thundered past.

"Oh," shuddered Little Snow Bear. "That made me so scared. They were huge!"

"There are plenty of things that are bigger," said his mother.

Next they came to a river. It splashed and crashed past them with a wild and mighty roaring.

"That's the biggest thing I've seen today," announced Little Snow Bear.

"Look at the mountain," said his mother gently. "See how far it goes."

The rocky mountain reached high into the sky. Little Snow Bear had to crane his neck to see the very top.

"But even that," she said softly, "is not the biggest thing in the world."

Further on, the river widened into the sea.

What was that noise?

Little Snow Bear turned just in time to see the tail
of a whale diving.

"That may not be the biggest thing in the world,"
he said firmly, "but it has the biggest tail."

"It probably has," said his mother.

As they sat by the shore, the wind rippled the water and a giant iceberg floated into view.

"It's very big," said Little Snow Bear. "Is *that* the biggest thing in the world?"

"Oh no," said his mother, nuzzling him close.

"I knew that," said Little Snow Bear, "because it's the sea, isn't it? The sea's bigger than anything else!"

"It's very, very, very big," said his mother. "But there's something bigger."

Little Snow
Bear wondered. As he
wondered, clouds gathered in the sky and
the wind blew more and more strongly.

With a sudden great *whoom*, the storm came. The last of the winter snow was falling in a whirl of icy flakes, and the storm was all around, huge and scary.

"Climb onto my back," whispered the mother bear to her cub.

Little Snow Bear climbed all the way up and lay down at last in her warm fur. He was rocked gently to sleep as she fought through the snow.

"It's how much I love you."

When he opened his eyes, everything was quiet once more. The sky was clear and dark, and a million stars shone.

"Oh," he whispered. "There's nothing bigger than that. There can't be."

"Come inside the den," his mother said, "and I will tell you what is bigger than anything else."

Lift the flap